I0759393

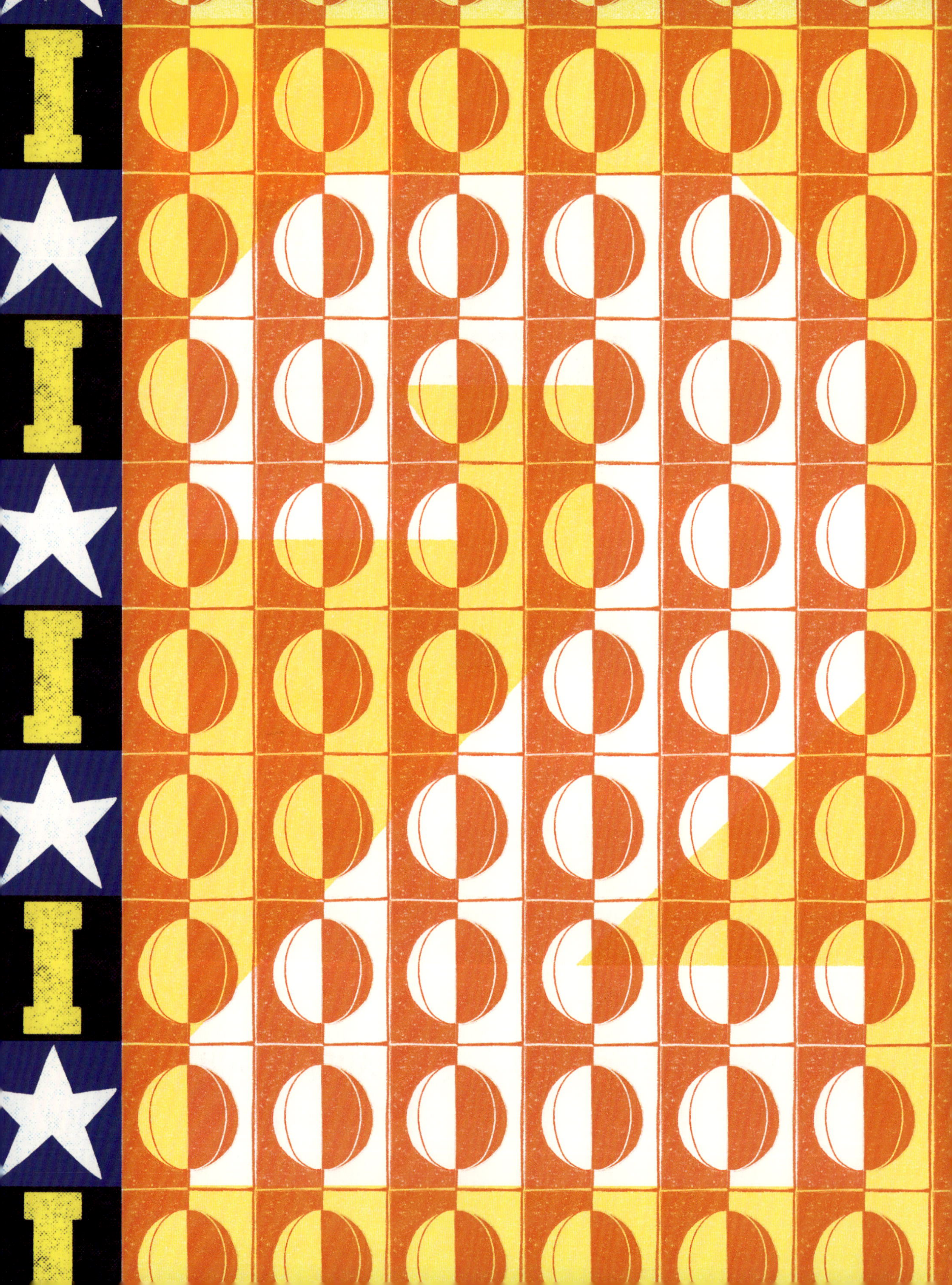

CAITLIN CLARK
Shooting Star
A BIOGRAPHY

by ERICA WAINER ★ illustrated by CLAUDIA MARIANNO

An Imprint of HarperCollinsPublishers

Caitlin Clark was born and raised in Iowa.

CLARK

It was in Iowa where, as a little kid,
Caitlin played soccer and softball,
track and basketball.
Even some golf.

She played sports with her brothers.

She joined them at their practices, dribbling beside them on courts and fields, playing one-and-one and learning the basics.

Caitlin practiced a lot because she did not like to lose— not to anyone, and especially not to her brothers!

Her dad became her first basketball coach.

Though Caitlin loved lots of sports,
basketball was her favorite.
And she had big plans for her basketball future.

Future Dreams

Be in the WNBA

To be STRONG

To live in a huge MANSION

To be in a basketball movie

To go on a basketball scholarship

To meet Maya Moore

College coaches from all across the United States began watching Caitlin play basketball when she was only in middle school. Halfway through high school, she began playing the sport exclusively.

Once, she scored sixty points in a single game (her team won).

Before long, Caitlin had a decision to make: Would she go away to college, to join one of the many coaches who had recruited her, or stay in Iowa?

IOWA
IOWA
GO HAWKS

Caitlin Clark stayed in Iowa.

She became a Hawkeye.

It would be one of the best decisions
Caitlin would make.

At Iowa, Caitlin started for the team as a freshman, and she shattered records for points and assists.

She didn't stop there.

Caitlin won . . .

. . . countless awards.

NANCY
LIEBERMAN
AWARD

B1G
Jostens

The Honda Cup
CLASS OF 2023
WOMAN ATHLETE
of the YEAR

DAWN STALEY AWARD

Caitlin worked hard.
She loved being in the gym.

Caitlin got stronger.
Bigger.
Faster.
She was unselfish on the court.
She was *very* competitive.

Her ability to score three-pointers
from almost nearly half-court
—called a Logo 3—
began to take on a life of its own.

Everyone wanted to watch Caitlin Clark shoot a basketball.

When Caitlin Clark was playing basketball with her dad and her brothers as a young girl in Iowa, she couldn't have imagined this:

55,646 people in Kinnick Stadium in Iowa City.

There to watch Caitlin.

The most people ever to watch a women's basketball game.

During Caitlin's senior year,
she became the NCAA's
all-time leading scorer.
For women.
And for men.

Caitlin helped her team reach the Final Four two years in a row. But the Hawkeyes didn't win the championship. Caitlin was disappointed.

Losing made her want to play smarter, practice more, and do better the next time.

As Caitlin's college career came to an end, she chose to join the WNBA.

Her dream had come true. Soon Caitlin would be getting paid to *play basketball* in a professional league, following many of her biggest heroes:

MAYA MOORE

JACKIE STILES

KELSEY PLUM

ELENA DELLE DONNE

Caitlin was drafted number one overall by the Indiana Fever.

In her first season in the WNBA, Caitlin and the Fever experienced highs and lows.

Caitlin was named Rookie of the Year, and the Fever made it to the playoffs for the first time since the 2016 season.

INDIANA
22
INDIANA
22
INDIANA
22

No matter if she is winning or losing,
Caitlin Clark finds joy in basketball.

Caitlin has so many eyes on her—and there are kids filling arenas and watching the game she plays and loves.

Buying her jerseys and her trading cards.
Designing her sneakers.
Imitating her three-point shot.

Being inspired by her determination,
her focus, her never-give-up attitude.

Caitlin Clark once played basketball in Des Moines, Iowa.
As a little kid, she played in driveways with her brothers
and practiced rebounding with her dad.
She played in high school gyms with her friends
and in college stadiums filled to the rafters,
where her number 22 is now retired.

Now Caitlin Clark plays basketball for all the world to see. The sky is the limit—with championships to win, records to break, and more dreams to fulfill.

FEVER
22

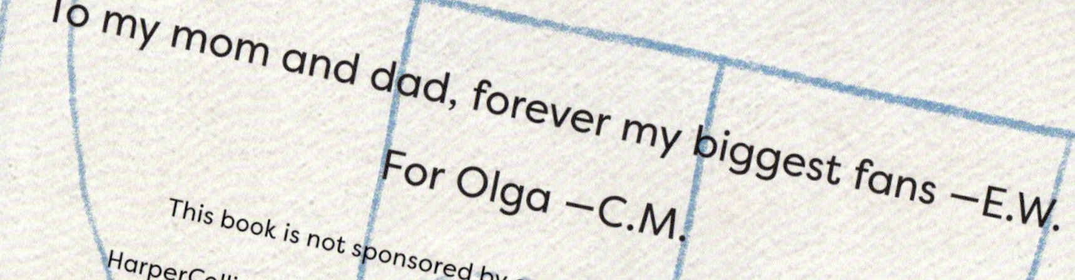

To my mom and dad, forever my biggest fans —E.W.

For Olga —C.M.

This book is not sponsored by or affiliated with Caitlin Clark.

HarperCollins Children's Books, a division of HarperCollins Publishers,
195 Broadway, New York, NY 10007

HarperCollins Publishers, Macken House, 39/40 Mayor Street Upper,
Dublin 1, D01 C9W8, Ireland

HarperPop is an imprint of HarperCollins Publishers.

Caitlin Clark: Shooting Star, A Biography

harpercollins.com

ISBN 978-0-06-345920-5

The artist used Photoshop to create the digital illustrations for this book.
Typography by Stephanie Hays
25 26 27 28 29 RTLO 10 9 8 7 6 5 4 3 2 1

First Edition

Sources

Baccellieri, E. "It's Been a Hell of a Year for Caitlin Clark." *Sports Illustrated*, October 3, 2024.

Caruso, S. "All About Caitlin Clark's Parents, Brent and Anne Nizzi-Clark." People.com, April 9, 2024. people.com/all-about-caitlin-clark-parents-8597994.

CBS News. "Caitlin Clark Passes 'Pistol' Pete Maravich's Record to Become All-Time NCAA Division I Scoring Leader." March 3, 2024. www.cbsnews.com/news/caitlin-clark-ncaa-division-1-record-pete-maravich.

Dougherty, S. "Photos: Iowa Star Caitlin Clark and Her Legion of Fans." *USA Today*, January 31, 2024.

ESPN Inside Look. "Caitlin Clark Tells Her Whole Hoops Story—From Childhood to Iowa to the WNBA Draft," interview by Holly Rowe. March 22, 2024. YouTube. www.youtube.com/watch?v=NOOZgZpKtog.

Lee, M. "Even as Chaos Swirls, Caitlin Clark Is Finding Joy in Her Rookie Year." *Washington Post*, June 13, 2024.

Lobo, R. "Growing the Game Is Caitlin Clark's Greatest Legacy." ESPN, April 15, 2024. www.espn.com/womens-college-basketball/story/_/id/39838971/caitlin-clark-iowa-scoring-record-legacy-college-career-ends.

Olson, E. "Caitlin Clark's 60-Point Game at Dowling Catholic Was a Sign of Things to Come." *Hawk Central*, February 6, 2024.

Rasmussen, K. "Caitlin Clark Has Powerful Response to Question About Inspiring Young Girls." *Sports Illustrated*, November 12, 2024.

Wikipedia. "Caitlin Clark." Last modified January 8, 2025. en.wikipedia.org/wiki/Caitlin_Clark.

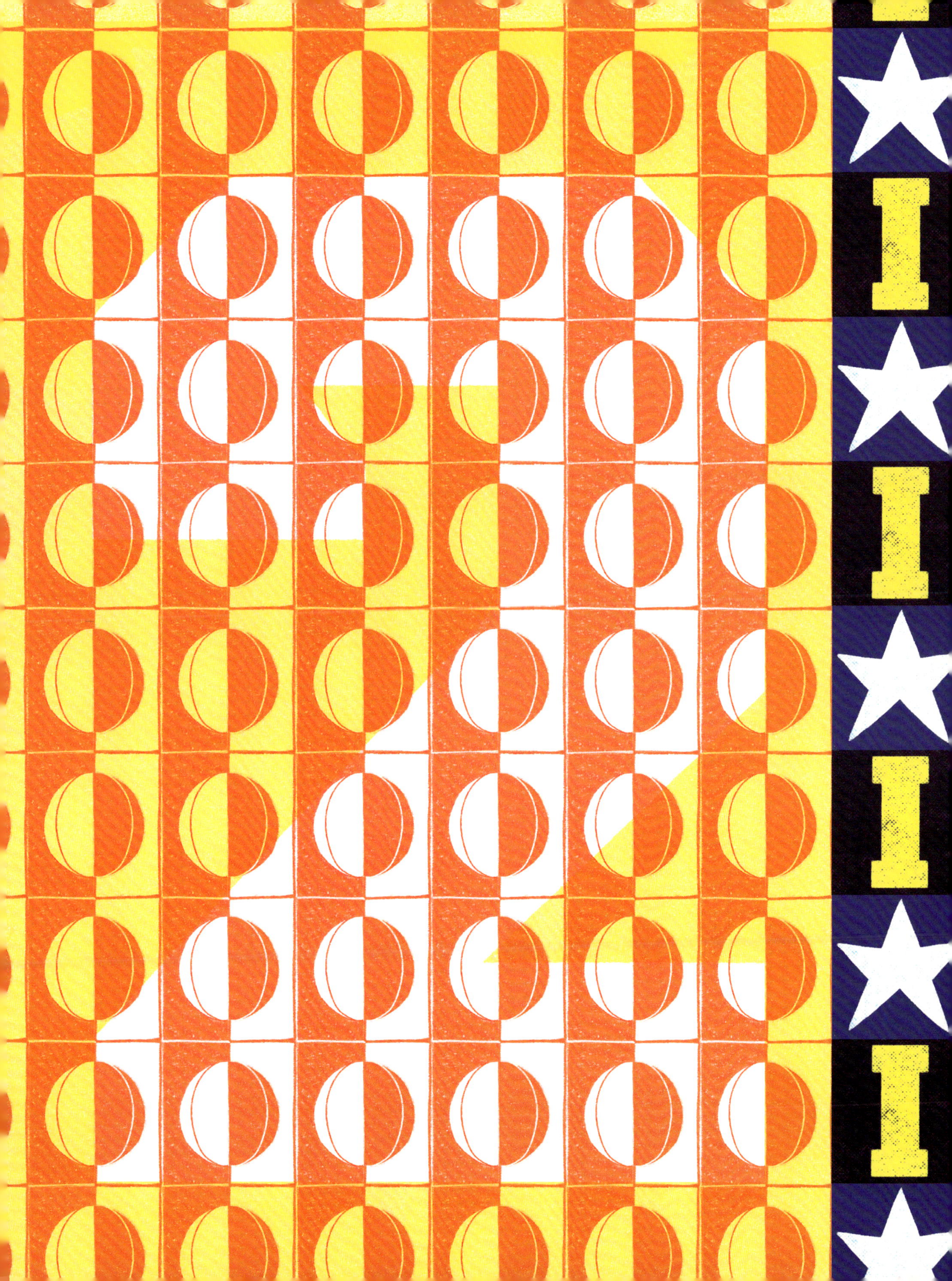

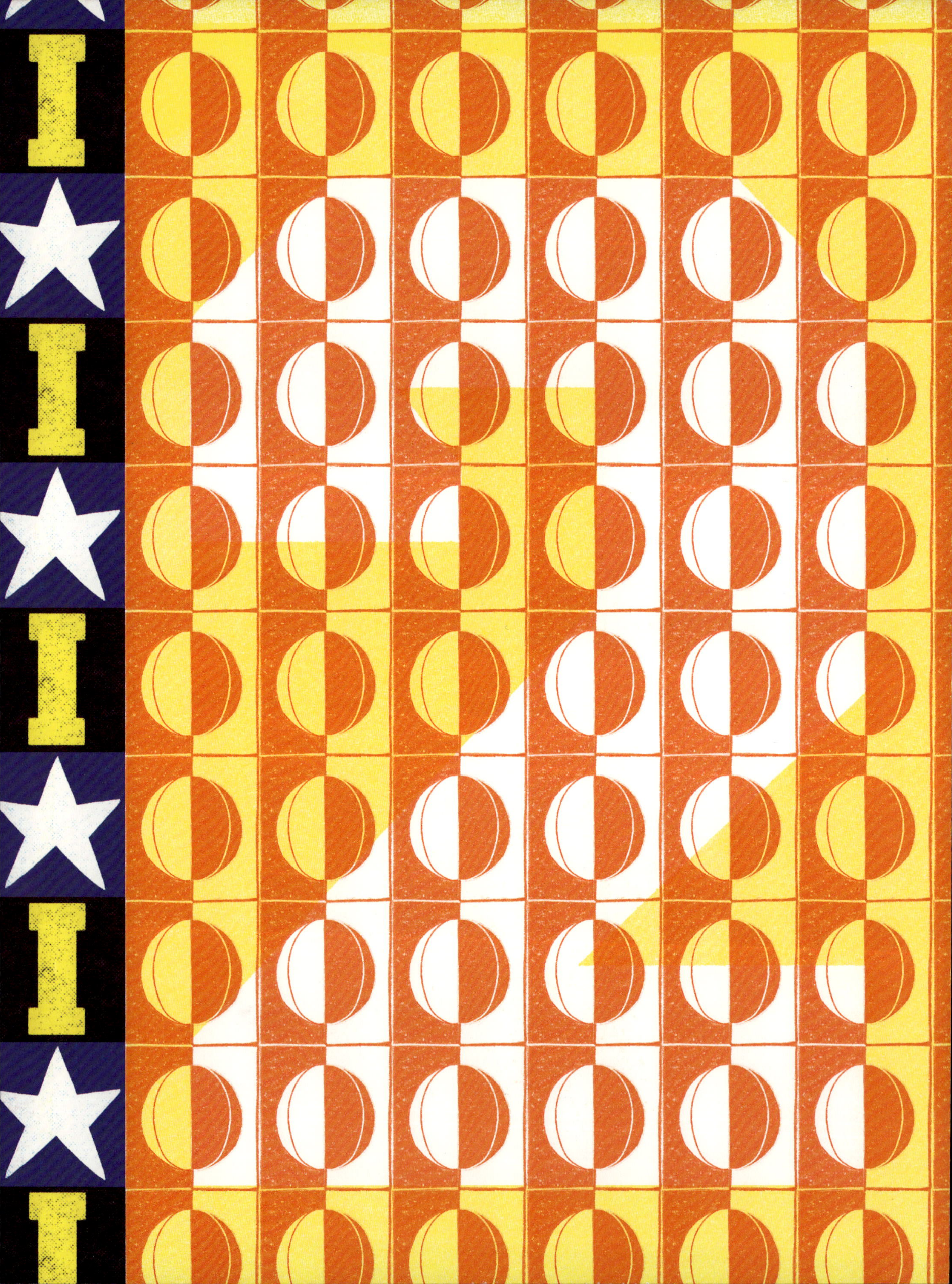